James the red engine, Edward, Henry, Percy, Toby and the Fat Controller, Sir Topham Hatt, who is in charge of all the engines.

The station is very busy and Thomas and his friends have many adventures which you can read about in this series. The stories are illustrated using colour photographs from the TV series.

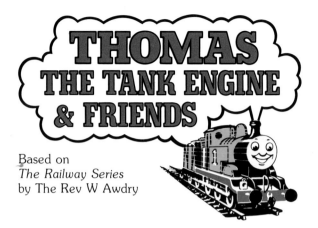

THOMAS THE TANK ENGINE & FRIENDS

Based on
The Railway Series
by The Rev W Awdry

Thomas and the missing Christmas tree
by Christopher Awdry
adapted from the television
story by Britt Allcroft
and David Mitton

Acknowledgments
*Photographic stills by David Mitton and Terry Permane
for Britt Allcroft Ltd. Additional photographs by Tim Clark*

British Library Cataloguing in Publication Data
Awdry, Christopher
    Thomas and the missing Christmas tree
    —(Thomas the tank engine and friends).
    I. Title   II. Series
    823'.914[J]   PZ7
    ISBN 0-7214-1051-0

First edition
© KAYE & WARD LTD 1984, 1986
© BRITT ALLCROFT LTD 1984, 1986
© In presentation LADYBIRD BOOKS LTD MCMLXXXVII

Printed in England

THOMAS
AND THE MISSING CHRISTMAS TREE

Ladybird Books

Every Christmas there is a carol concert on the Island of Sodor. The town band plays and lots of people come to sing carols round the Christmas tree.

Afterwards there is always a special treat for the children and, this year, the Fat Controller wants the party to be an extra special celebration...

Thomas and the
missing Christmas tree

It was two days before the carol concert. The Fat Controller was very busy giving orders for everywhere to be scrubbed and polished, ready for the special night.

The engines were all very excited. They had been helping with the preparations and now Henry, Gordon and Thomas were waiting at the station for the Fat Controller to give them their final orders.

"You all have jobs to do," said the Fat Controller. "Henry," he said, importantly, "you are in charge of the cards, letters and parcels. Gordon, you will bring the Mayor."

The Fat Controller paused impressively, "And Thomas... you will have the most Important Job. I want you to fetch the Christmas tree. Duck will look after Annie and Clarabel until you get back."

Thomas beamed with pride.

"Yes, sir," he said. "Will we be able to sing the carols, too?"

"We'll see," promised the Fat Controller.

That night the other engines sulked in their shed.

"Why should Thomas go?" grumbled Henry. "He can't do anything a splendid green engine like me couldn't do."

"Nor me," agreed Gordon. "Anyone would think he was special or something."

But Thomas didn't care what they said. *He* had been picked for the most Important Job.

"You're only jealous," he said. And he shut his eyes and went to sleep.

Next morning, Thomas set off to fetch the Christmas tree. "It would be nice to sing carols again," he sighed as he puffed along on his important mission.

Thomas had to go down the line through Edward's station to pick up the tree. The Fat Controller had said that Thomas had to be back by teatime.

Thomas picked up the tree safely and set off on the return journey. "I mustn't be late," he thought. "The Fat Controller is relying on me."

But it had been snowing again. Large
snow drifts lay ahead and Thomas was
not wearing his snowplough. He whistled
bravely and tried to make his way
through. He ran into a snow drift and
tried to turn his wheels, but it was no
good – he was stuck.

Suddenly the wind blew the snow all
over him. Thomas was snowed under!

Back at the station it had been snowing, too. The workmen rushed off to fetch their shovels to clear a path for the visitors.

The other engines waited for Thomas to come back. They waited and waited.

"Perhaps he's stuck in a tunnel

somewhere?" suggested Gordon.

Henry let off steam indignantly. "Pooh!" he said. "He's much more likely to have been turned onto the branch line."

"He could have run into a cow..." suggested Donald.

"Silence!" said the Fat Controller. "We know that Thomas collected the tree safely, but now the snow has brought down the telephone wires. We must assume that Thomas is stranded somewhere near Edward's station."

The engines all felt sorry for poor Thomas.

"We're not going to leave him there, sir, are we?" asked Douglas.

"Certainly not," said the Fat Controller. "I will need two volunteers to go and find Thomas."

All the engines hooted at once! They all wanted to help to rescue Thomas. The twins, Donald and Douglas, were chosen for the job.

Quickly the men fetched the snowploughs and the driver and fireman checked each one to see that everything was ready for the journey.

Soon Donald and Douglas set off to the rescue, feeling cold but confident.

"Good luck," the other engines whistled as the twins left the yard.

At the junction, they met Toby, Percy and Duck.

"The Fat Controller has cancelled all trains until Thomas is found," said Duck. "So take care."

"Come back safely with Thomas and the missing Christmas tree!" added Toby, giving a final blast on his whistle, just for luck.

Donald and Douglas puffed bravely
on, but the snow was getting thicker
now. They struggled through Edward's
station.

Donald wanted to stop for a rest but
Douglas wouldn't let him, "What if Thomas

is lying hurt somewhere?" he said.

Great snowdrifts lay across Gordon's hill. Again and again Donald and Douglas forced the snowploughs into the deep snow, and each time they managed to move slowly forward.

Then they drew back and paused for breath.

"What's that?" hissed Douglas. "I can hear something!"

Very faintly, there came a muffled cry. "Help! Help!"

"Probably the wind," insisted Donald.

"No, listen," said Douglas.

"Help! Over here!"

"Och! It's Thomas," they cried together.

"Come on," said Douglas. "Let's get him out — he must be frozen to his frames in there."

The men began to dig the snow away. Thomas's driver and fireman, who had taken shelter in a nearby cottage, came out to help too. It was not long before they had dug Thomas *and* the missing Christmas tree out of the snow.

Thomas was pleased to see the twins but he was feeling cold and miserable. The men coupled him up behind Donald and Douglas and they all set off on their journey home.

When the engines arrived at the station, everyone gave Thomas such a

warm welcome that he began to feel quite cheerful again.

The Christmas tree was quickly unloaded, put into its tub and decorated for the carol concert. There was a great rush to get the station ready and by the time the Mayor and visitors came crowding in, everything looked splendid.

The Fat Controller stood in front of the engines. "As a reward for all your hard work today," he said, smiling, "you may go and enjoy the carols. Be quick now!"

"Yes, sir," said all the engines.

"Wheesh!" said James, letting off steam because he was so pleased. The Fat Controller paused. "Kindly remember that this is a special occasion. Be on your best behaviour and I want no ...er... 'wheeshing', please."

The engines took their places at the carol concert.

"One! Two! Three!" boomed the Fat Controller. And suddenly, as if by magic, the station was flooded with light. And there was the Christmas tree, decorated with coloured lamps, stars and lights!

Then the Fat Controller shouted, "Three cheers for Thomas the Tank Engine and his friends." And everyone clapped and cheered.

The engines were delighted. James was

so excited that he let out a great "wheesh!" Everyone laughed, and this time not even the Fat Controller seemed to mind very much.

Suddenly there was a strange whirring noise. It seemed to come from the sky and there, with his landing lights shining brightly, was Harold the Helicopter. He came down gently in the snow, and out stepped a figure wearing a red cloak.

Everyone cheered. It was Father Christmas!

He handed out presents to all the children, and thanked

the engines for rescuing Thomas and
saving the missing Christmas tree.
"Happy Christmas, Thomas, and to all
your friends," he said.

The carol party was a great success.
Afterwards Thomas and Percy went back
to the shed together.

"It's no fun getting stuck in the snow,"
whispered Thomas to Percy. "But it·was
worth it for the party. Happy Christmas,
Percy. Happy Christmas, everyone."